The Treasure of Cosy Cove

A Red Fox Book

Published by Random Century Children's Books
20 Vauxhall Bridge Road, London SW1V 2SA

A division of the Random Century Group
London Melbourne Sydney Auckland
Johannesburg and agencies throughout the world

First published by Andersen Press Ltd 1989

Red Fox edition 1991
© Tony Ross 1989

Printed and bound in Hong Kong

ISBN 0 09 972770 6

The Treasure of
Cosy Cove

or
The Voyage of the "Kipper"

Tony Ross

RED FOX

"Help!" squealed Smudge.
"Mother save us!" squeaked Kitty. "I can't waterpaddle."

The kittens hit the water – and sank and sank –

until their cheeks were bursting and everything was dark. Suddenly strong paws pulled them up again.

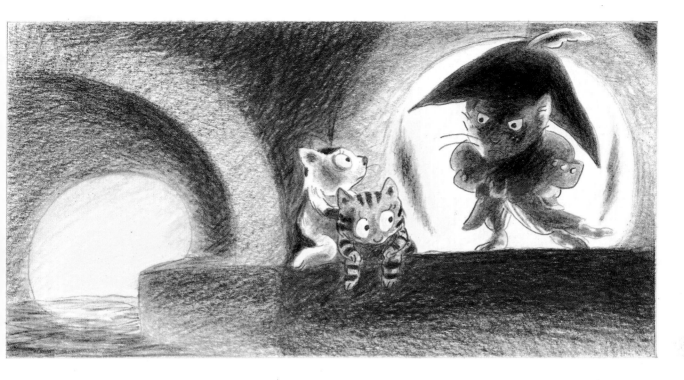

"A lucky escape, me hearties," growled a shadowy figure with strong paws.

"Follow me!" and the two kittens followed him. Down twisty dank tunnels and ways filled with sudden frights.

They followed along the dock walls, down secret holes

and up hidden stairs to a trap door and warm room. At last, the ginger cat spoke again. "I'm Israel Claws, Cap'n Claws, and here's where I rest me whiskers."

The Cap'n dried the kittens and they all had fishtails and custard for supper.

Then Smudge and Kitty were given warm clothes. Proper clothes for being by the water. "AHA, lads," growled the Cap'n. "You're all ship-shape now. Time for a yarn, I'm thinking."

Reaching into a hidey hole, the Cap'n pulled out a piece of paper. "It's a map, lads," he whispered. "A chart…

I took it years ago, from a seadog too tired to fight. It shows the way to the wonderful treasure of Cosy Cove. Now I've found a crew, we can sail tomorrow." That night, the kittens dreamed of treasure.

Early next morning, the Cap'n went in search of a boat.

He went to Tom Tars Tavern, where the badcats gathered to sing. "Belay!" he shouted above the din. "Me and these two lads is looking for a ship and we've good money to spend."

But nobody had a boat to sell. Suddenly, the room went quiet…

as a fearsome figure hopped forward on three wooden legs. "It's Tiddles 'Awkins!" someone gasped. "The baddest badcat in the Drain. Some says the big fish took 'is legs!"

"I've just the ship for you, sir," purred 'Awkins. "Just 'op this way."

Tiddles 'Awkins led the three adventurers down the tunnels as fast as his leg would carry him. At last, he stopped, puffed and pointed. "There she lies. I calls 'er the *Kipper*!"

Cap'n Claws and the crew liked the *Kipper* and bought her.

They prepared to sail at once. Nobody noticed Tiddles 'Awkins hide inside an empty barrel. He could SMELL treasure and decided to get it for himself.

The wind was in the right direction, the tide was just right and the Cap'n steered the little boat out into the open water. A cheer went up as the sails filled. The voyage of the *Kipper* had begun!

When darkness fell, 'Awkins climbed out of the barrel.

Smudge was asleep at the tiller and didn't notice as 'Awkins sneaked into the cabin. Quiet as a clam, he slid the map from the Cap'n's trouser pocket and sneaked out again.

"TREASURE!" cackled 'Awkins, hopping back into his barrel.

But sound carries through water and deep below the *Kipper*, something moved.
The big fish heard the cackling and the voice reminded him of breakfast.

All night, the big fish followed...

and at first light, attacked. "Fish ahoy!" yelled Kitty. Smudge and the Cap'n rushed to see.

"All paws to the barrel!" ordered the Cap'n.

As the big fish flopped over the side of the ship, the crew heaved the barrel into the terrible mouth. The big fish slid back into the deeps, taking the rest of Tiddles 'Awkins with him.

The *Kipper* sailed on, through fair weather and foul.

The Cap'n steered clear of many dangers, until from the top of the mast, the lookout called: "DOG HO! SEADOG OFF THE PORT BOW!"

The seadog almost sank the *Kipper*, but the cats fought him off.

"Quick!" shouted the Cap'n. "Head for that hole. He'll not follow us there." Just in the nick of time, the *Kipper* sailed into a dark drain – only to come out...

… in the park boating pond! The seadog found the pond too, but couldn't find the *Kipper* amongst the model yachts. When it was safe the *Kipper* slipped away.

At last, they could go no further. Their way was barred by massive walls and wooden gates.

"Sorry, mates," moaned the Cap'n. "Seems we're stuck. Seems I've lost the map too." As he spoke, water poured out of the stone walls, the *Kipper* stood on end and the crew was washed overboard.

The Cap'n, the crew and the *Kipper* were pulled down into the deeps. It was like water going down a plughole. Their clothes were swirled away and they couldn't breathe. Everything ended in the dark. Quietness.

In the cold early morning, an old woman found two kittens…

and an old cat, lying in the mud. They were more dead than alive. The woman
took them home with her and warmed them by the fire.

The old woman loved the cats and decided to keep them.

"It's nice here, she's nice and it's good to have a home," sighed Smudge. "But I'm sad we never found the treasure of Cosy Cove." The Cap'n winked, then yawned...

... he'd explain in the morning.

Other titles in the Red Fox picture book series (incorporating Beaver Books)